~~Karen~~ & ~~Hooper~~

17 Dempster Street

~~Wick~~

~~Post~~ ~~code~~ ~~KW14QB~~

T.E.L ~~3454~~

Dangerous
Journey

Cover illustration by **Francis Phillipps**

Inside the book . . .

Jane Ettridge illustrated "Dangerous Journey", "Rustlers on the Moor", "Coming Up Trumps" and "Circus Tricks".

Valerie Sangster illustrated "Catch as Catch Can".

Dudley Wynne illustrated "The Empty Field", "Count Your Blessings", "A Spectacular Pony", "Champions", "The Lie" and "The Search".

AWARD PONY STORIES

Dangerous Journey

...and other pony stories

ROSEMARY SIMMONDS

AWARD PUBLICATIONS

ISBN 0-86163-340-7

Copyright © 1989 Award Publications Limited

First published 1989

Published by Award Publications Limited,
Spring House, Spring Place
Kentish Town, London NW5 3BH

Printed in the GDR

CONTENTS

Marie-Louise urged her pony on

Dangerous Journey

A rrow bounced beneath the saddle, her head pulling up against the restraining leather of the martingale. Nicholas Shaw held the reins firmly in his left hand. In his right was a willow-wood mallet. His eyes focused on a small white ball some fifty metres from him. He counted beneath his breath.

"Three... two... " he must not touch Arrow until the perfect moment, "one... go!" His rein hand moved forward and the roan mare leapt away. Nicholas swung the mallet up and out behind him. He timed the move perfectly to catch the ball sideways so that it cut an arc across the mare's chest before hurtling over the dusty ground.

Arrow wheeled round instantly, following the ball. Nicholas brought her up on the right this time and leaned across the saddle to hit a backhand shot far down the airstrip. Arrow needed only a touch on the rein to spin round and pursue the ball with long, hungry strides.

In his mind, Nicholas was running ivory poachers off the savannah.

The ball hit a tussock of grass, bounced and came to rest. Nicholas drew rein, dismounted and put the ball in his pocket. Arrow hung her head, breathing heavily. Her nostrils were wide and red-centred.

Nicholas ran the stirrups up and slipped the leathers over the irons to secure them. He loosened the girth and took the reins over the mare's head to lead her back to the farm.

Dangerous Journey

Nicolas timed the move to perfection

It was at times like these that Arrow's seventeen years began to show. She had been twelve when his father gave her to him. Nicholas remembered how he had barely been able to reach the saddle. There was a lot he did not know then.

Why, he had even believed his father's story that her unusual colouring had been caused by the Maasai dying her coat with red ochre and chalk as they did their own skins. He laughed at himself and patted the mare's neck. She was just an old polo pony from Nairobi, nothing more unusual than that.

Arrow picked her head up and whickered to the other horses in the paddock. Marie-Louise's Arab pony, Turk, answered with a friendly neigh. Logic and Darling continued to graze their way towards the umbrella-like shade of the acacia trees where they would spend the heat of the day standing nose to tail, swishing away persistent flies.

Would his sister play polo when she came home for the holidays? Nicholas wondered. He needed someone to practise riding against. It was not that he was particularly keen on the game, but if he could impress his parents with his skill in the saddle by scoring a few goals, he might be able to persuade them to change their minds about not allowing him to ride onto the savannah below. It was all down to getting enough practice and that depended upon Marie-Louise.

After turning Arrow loose, Nicholas showered and changed into white shorts and a shirt. His mother called him to hurry, reminding him that they must be at the airport by one. Nicholas pushed his feet into sandals and paused to give a biscuit to the chameleon on the windowledge. His parrot reminded him to "Have a nice day" as he dashed from the room.

At the screen door Nicholas paused, called back by the cook who held out a vacuum flask. "Freshly squeezed orange juice," she said. "Chilled just as your mother likes it."

"What would I do without you!" Nicholas said with genuine feeling.

Cook laughed, flashing strong white teeth. "Forget your own head, I shouldn't wonder," she chuckled as Nicholas leapt off the verandah and jogged to the waiting car.

"Must you run everywhere," complained Mrs. Shaw as her son climbed into the Range-Rover beside her. "We have not yet left home and you are

already covered in dust."

"Sorry," said Nicholas.

His mother slammed the car into gear, pushed Beethoven's 5th Symphony into the cassette player and turned the volume up very loud. Nicholas stared out of the window, watching the roadside thorn trees and dry grasses flash by, while in the distance the mountains barely moved.

Two hours to get to Nairobi, another hour waiting for Marie-Louise at the airport, then over to their father's office and a bite to eat before coming home again. A whole day wasted when he could have been watching the springbok herd from the end of the airstrip. By tomorrow, they would have moved on and he would not be able to get a good view even with binoculars.

Nicholas thought of Arrow. The mare would be perfect to use for tracking. She was intelligent and brave. He had taught her to move soundlessly, placing each hoof with care, barely breathing, her tail hanging motionless.

Gates along the side of the road showed they were now passing the edge of a game reserve. If only he could have spent the day there. His father's world of offices, business deals and international finance did not appeal to Nicholas. He wanted to work on the reserve when he left school, but his parents would not hear of it. Now, they were even talking about sending him away to a boarding school in England.

The flight was half-an-hour late.

Dangerous Journey

The car sped on whilst, in the back Nicholas was busy with his dreams

Nicholas sat on a plastic chair in the airport lounge and felt the seat stick to him. There would be red marks on the back of his legs when he stood up. He hated that. At last the doors opened and Marie-Louise came through the arrivals gate. Nicholas hurried to help with her luggage. "Did you have a good flight, darling?" Mrs. Shaw asked, kissing her daughter's cheek.

They went on to Mr. Shaw's office, where sandwiches and tea were brought in by the secretary. Marie-Lousie reported that she had been made captain of the netball team and this pleased her parents. Then, she handed over a sealed brown envelope containing the end-of-year reports. Nicholas exchanged a grim smile of commiseration with his sister.

"Will you do some polo practice with me?" Nicholas asked his sister as they drove back. "I need to get Arrow used to riding against other horses."

"Polo? Who dreamed that up?" asked Marie-Louise.

"School, though I don't know why – but will you?" persisted Nicholas.

"I'll never hit the ball," laughed Marie-Louise.

"That doesn't matter," exclaimed Nicholas. "Just gallop after it!"

Marie-Louise blanched. "I'm not even sure I can still do that," she explained. "In England, we have our lessons in a covered school mostly. It's all heels down, change the rein and make one's teeth rattle with sitting trot."

But she did manage to do all that

Nicholas expected of her. Within ten minutes of being in the saddle, all her old skills had come back and Turk was galloping so fast the wind brought tears to her eyes. They pulled up, laughing. Turk bowed his head and coughed. His coat was speckled with white and was soapy to the touch.

"He is terribly unfit," said Marie-Louise. She stretched her arms behind her, adding: "And so am I – my shoulders will pay for this gallop tomorrow morning."

They rode back on a loose rein. Marie-Louise pointed to their mother reading the fashion pages of London magazines she had brought with her on the flight. She was sitting in the thatched summer house on the far side of the lawn, with her feet stretched in front of her and looking unusually relaxed.

"Can you really do fancy shots?" Marie-Louise asked, returning to the subject of polo.

"Roll the ball and I'll show you,"

Riding back on a loose rein

invited Nicholas, smiling confidently.

Marie-Louise threw the ball out, but Arrow ignored it. Her sixth sense had alerted her to nearby danger. Nicholas reacted automatically, his muscles trembling with pent-up energy. Then he saw it, winding out of the thatch not far from his mother. It was a black mamba with head curling back and ready to spit.

There was no time to think. His knees held him tight to the saddle as Arrow sped across the forbidden lawn. Nicholas brought his arm back and then swung the mallet forward. The mamba flew through the air, to drop limply among the flower pots.

"Nicholas!" his mother cried as she jumped to her feet. Her face was white. "You could have provoked it to strike!"

She sat down abruptly. Her face crumpled and she started to cry.

Marie-Louise jumped off her pony and waved him away.

"I'm sorry I shouted, Nicholas," said his mother when she came to his room

later. 'It was all such a shock. You were very brave. I am proud of you."

"I wasn't really," shrugged Nicholas. "There wasn't time to be brave."

"Nevertheless . . ." she gave a little smile. "Your father is bringing some business friends back from Nairobi for the weekend. I had hoped he would have been able to take you and Marie-Louise out to Lake Baringo, but that doesn't seem very likely now. Perhaps you would like to take your sister to see the antelope instead."

"In the valley?" asked Nicholas, trying to hide his excitement.

"Yes, but do be careful," smiled his mother.

Next morning, Nicholas and his sister were up at seven and feasting on a breakfast of paw-paws sprinkled with lime juice, eggs, bacon and lashings of toast. The horses were given long enough to digest an extra large breakfast and then the two of them set out, with stirrup leathers lengthened for long hours in the saddle and hats tipped to shade the sun.

Their path led down from the highlands between regular fields of coffee and sissal to the spreading plain. They caught up with the springbok not far out and followed them for an hour before turning south to track a family of giraffe.

As the sun began to gain height, Marie-Louise pulled her horse to a halt and announced: "That's far enough!"

"Just a little further," Nicholas pleaded, loathe to leave the savannah.

"Turk is not fit and there is a long ride back," said Marie-Louise in sympathy with her mount.

"You can wait here for me and I'll go on alone," insisted Nicholas.

"We shouldn't split up," was his sister's wise reminder. "It's dangerous!"

"I promise I won't go far," promised Nicholas. "Half-an-hour, no longer. I have my compass, I won't get lost."

"Oh, all right," Marie-Louise agreed grudgingly, "but not a minute more and stay within sight!"

Nicholas trotted away. This was what he had dreamed of, riding alone in the valley, with only himself and the animals. It would be like this in the future, if ever he became a game warden. He must make his father see how much he really meant to become a warden. He would work very hard at biology and then they would *have* to think of him taking a job with animals.

Arrow stiffened and lifted her head to sniff the air. Nicholas began to tremble. He wished his parents had let him carry a gun. In the undergrowth, twigs cracked.

A lion?

Arrow paddled the ground, her ears pricked and standing tall like twin sentries. Nicholas ran his tongue over his lip and tasted salt. A shadow moved behind the leaves. Branches whipped back. A black muzzle appeared, followed by a striped body and a stubby tail.

Nicholas let his jaw drop as he relaxed back into the saddle. The

Nicholas began to tremble until he realised what had made the sudden noise

zebra foal gave a shrill neigh, recognizing the scent of horse, but knowing it was not quite right. Arrow lowered her head to give a deep, maternal whicker. The foal hesitated, then came towards her. The near hind leg was stiff and it limped badly.

The foal should have been with its mother, thought Nicholas, yet they had not seen zebra all morning. Somehow, it must have got separated from the herd, caught in the bushes perhaps. That would explain the gash around the foal's hock that was causing the limp.

Without touching the rein, Nicholas asked the roan to go forward. Arrow took three steps. The foal bobbed along beside her. Could he take it home? A lame zebra might draw danger to them. It was the perfect prey for a hungry leopard or hyena. His father said nature wrote her own rules and they should not interfere with them.

The game wardens would probably say the same – observe, but do not

intrude. Nicholas knew though that he could not abandon the creature, he simply could not!

"Mother will have a blue fit when she sees it," said Marie-Louise when he eventually reached her. "She'll tell you it is wrong as well as illegal and dangerous and that you're bringing disease onto the farm. For crying out loud, Nick, how are you going to get a wild zebra through the plantations?"

"I'm not," Nicholas told her. "I am going to go up the gully and along the airstrip." He spoke with quiet determination, his protective instincts roused. After all, the foal only needed a little time to heal itself and then it could go back to the plains. Nicholas didn't plan to make a pet out of it. He knew better than that.

By the time they reached the farm, the foal was too exhausted to worry about the strange new environment. Nicholas put Arrow into a loose-box away from the other horses and brought her water and a little hay.

His father was waiting for him on the verandah. Marie-Louise was there too, her fingers knotted together, her cheeks flushed.

"You should have left the animal where it belongs," his father growled. "I shall have to get Mr. Onyango to come out and take a look at it. You do realize that you have stolen that foal, don't you, Nicholas?"

"But. . ." began Nicholas.

"No buts," snapped his father. "What would happen if everyone helped themselves to the animals? Now, off you go and clean up. I want you looking decent when Mr. Onyango arrives."

Mr. Onyango was the chief warden on the reserve. Nicholas chewed his fingernails as he watched the khaki Land-Rover sweep over the brow and along the drive. His father would tell the story first and make him appear in the wrong. Then, the warden would be annoyed with him and he would never get to work on the reserve. He wished he had never set eyes on the zebra foal.

The two men shook hands and walked towards the house. "So this is the culprit," said Mr. Onyango as Nicholas came to the edge of the verandah. He dug his hands into his pockets and then pulled them out again, remembering that his mother had told him it was impolite.

"There's no need for you to trouble yourself further, Mr. Shaw," said the warden. "Your son can direct me to the stable."

As they walked to the side of the house, Mr. Onyango made Nicholas repeat his tale of how he had come upon the foal. When they reached the box, he stood a moment and rested his arms on the bottom door while observing the young zebra.

"He's old enough to be weaned," he murmured, "so that's one problem less to worry about. Now, let's see to that injured leg."

Mr. Onyango took a syringe out of his bag. "This will reduce the swelling

Dangerous Journey

They stood for a moment observing the young zebra

and keep the wound clear of infection," he told Nicholas. "I'll need you to hold him. Will you help?"

Nicholas nodded. "Just tell me what to do," he said.

The warden did not waste any time. As soon as Nicholas caught the foal's head, he injected its neck. It was all over in a matter of seconds.

"I'll be back in a few days to see how the foal is coming on," said Mr. Onyango. "We may be able to re-introduce him to the wild without too much trouble, as long as the herd will accept him. Make sure he doesn't get too attached to you." The warden smiled and added: "I'm afraid you may have to ignore your horse for a while."

"She'll have to get used to that," Nicholas explained. "I'm going to boarding school in England after the summer."

"Off to learn how to follow in your father's footsteps?" smiled Mr. Onyango.

"I'd rather follow in yours," said

Nicholas and then flushed, cursing his impulsiveness for the second time that day.

Mr. Onyango laughed. "So, you like the idea of going on safari," he said. They had reached the house by now and Nicholas's father was waiting to invite Mr. Onyango indoors for a drink before he left. "I'm afraid I must hurry," the warden apologised, but had time to add: "Perhaps your son would like to spend part of his holiday on the reserve – give him some first-hand training so he knows what to do next time."

He winked at Nicholas and the boy smiled back. Suddenly, next term and England seemed years away.

The Empty
Field

Lee Copeland took the lane from Gorselands Farm to the barley field and then climbed over the gate to walk along the narrow path that ran beside the hedge. His fingers played with the halter rope as he walked. Mr. Randall had pointed out a rough corner behind the barns that he could clear and use for schooling.

Lee had spent all of Saturday cutting the grass back and chasing up barrels and planks that he could use to make jumps. He had four built now, quite sizeable ones, and he could not wait to try the palomino over them.

Lee hurried along. That was why he had picked Golden Nugget out, not for his colour but for his rubber-ball jumping ability. The summer shows were just coming round. This time he would be amongst the prizewinners. Lee smiled confidently as he imagined the names of himself and Golden Nugget printed beneath a black and white photograph in the Harsley and District Gazette.

The bottom of the long field opened onto a sloping paddock. Lee climbed onto the gate and cupped his hands to his mouth. "Nugget!" he called, but there was no response.

"Nugget!" he called again and felt his heart begin to race. This was the third time in a week! Lee jumped down and ran to the brow from where he could see the whole of the field. It was empty.

"Impossible animal!" Lee muttered, slapping the ground with the lead rope.

Where would the insufferable horse be this time? At Ayton probably, five miles away in one of the three racing stables that bordered the town. Lee plodded back up the field. He ought to be hurrying, but he was weary of these hunts. Yet another day to waste running about trying to find the horse – a day he could have spent riding.

Back home, Lee's mother was in the kitchen, beating eggs to go into a coffee cake for their Bank Holiday tea. She looked at her son's face, then at the kitchen clock and said: "Not again?"

"Yes, again!" Lee replied heavily.

Mrs. Copeland shook her head. "That horse is more trouble than it is worth," she said. "Mr. Randall won't be pleased about this."

"You don't need to tell me that!" Lee snapped. He had already been warned by the farmer that Nugget would have to be tethered if he got loose again. Lee did not dare tether the palomino because he was too excitable and down in that sloping field, out of sight of the

Lee's mother knew at once something was wrong

farm, he could get tangled in the rope and no-one would know about it.

Lee picked up the telephone receiver and dialled the first of the three stables. Nugget had made a nuisance of himself at one of them when he'd found the feed room door open and gorged himself on oats. Mr. Mackay said he was lucky not to have had a fatal dose of colic from the feast.

Nugget was not at Mackay's, nor Lyndhurst, nor Treetham Stables. Lee put the receiver back in its cradle. A nervous sweat prickled along his brow. Maybe Nugget had been in an accident? Perhaps he should call the police. His fingers stretched for the telephone again, then stopped. If the police learned that the horse frequently went missing, they might say that he was unfit to keep it and take Nugget away from him!

Lee decided he would go and look himself first, as maybe the horse had simply got itself lost in the woods and was just waiting for rescue.

Lee got out his bicycle and pedalled along all the local lanes, shouting Nugget's name. The minutes ticked away. An hour went by and he was no closer to finding the horse. Reluctantly, Lee turned back towards home.

His heart was heavy and he realized why he had been so reticent to call the police. It was like admitting that Nugget might be dead, that there had been a horrible accident. The road from Killerby was busy at the best of times and this was a holiday weekend. Lee put his bicycle by the wall, licked dry lips and steeled himself to make the phone call that would tell him the truth when he got indoors.

As it happened, his mother made the call. She seemed to think he would get muddled up. Lee hung back by the kitchen door, listening and correcting her description. He was just about to mention the horse's single white sock when his mother shook her hand and made a scribbling motion on the air to send him in search of a pen and notepad.

"Twenty-nine, Grove Lane, Barrowby," she said as she wrote the words down. "Thank you for your help."

His mother replaced the receiver and handed the note to Lee. "He's gone in a different direction this time," she told him. "You had better go and fetch him right away. I'll call Mrs.Sibson to let her know you are on your way. Her daughter caught him – she's called Philippa."

It was a long walk through three

miles of winding lane. Lee was thirsty by the time he turned into the drive of number twenty-nine. He hoped they had not had too much trouble with the horse and then they might offer him a cold drink and a rest before he started for home.

The front door opened as he reached it and an eleven-year-old girl with blonde plaits and a wide smile jumped onto the step. "Lee Copeland?" she asked.

"Yes — is Nugget here?" asked Lee. He looked around him at the tidy little lawn with its flower borders and wondered how Nugget had ever decided to come to this house.

"He's round the back," Philippa told him. "I wasn't sure if he would be safe to tether, so I put him in Jubilee's stable." Philippa led the way through a small gap between the house and the garage. There was a thin strip of lawn with plenty of flowers along the border — some even climbing up the garden fence, making a good display.

Lee did not miss the dents made by four large hoofs. Nugget stuck his head out of the timber stable, which he dwarfed to the dimensions of a shed, and whinnyed. The small black pony tied beside the door turned its head to look at the newcomer. "I hope he hasn't caused too much trouble," said Lee, aware of the reverence people like his father paid to their lawns.

Philippa shook her head. "He heard Jubilee calling for her breakfast I think," she smiled. "Did he break out of the field?"

Nugget stuck his head out of the small stable and whinnyed

"He jumped out!" Lee told her and sighed as he patted the palomino's neck. "You are very naughty, you know," he told the horse and then turned back to tell Philippa: "Usually he goes to the racing stables at Ayton. Mr. Randall's mad at me because he keeps flattening the crops, but I can't keep him in."

Philippa nodded in sympathy. She watched the palomino reach over the door and rub noses with Jubilee. "Have you had Nugget long?" she asked.

"Three weeks," sighed Lee, and then Philippa asked where Nugget had come from.

"Mrs. Layton – she has a riding school over at Killerby," Lee told her. "Do you know it?" Philippa nodded. She had been there for lessons before she bought Jubilee. It was a huge place with over thirty horses, an indoor school big enough to get lost in and a permanent cross-country course. "Maybe Nugget's lonely," she suggested.

Lonely? Lee blinked, but it made

sense. He'd been thinking so much about the quality of the grass, or mischief on Nugget's part, that he'd overlooked the obvious. After all, horses were herd animals and at the school Nugget had been used to running amongst a tribe of his friends whenever he was turned out.

"Do you have space for another pony in your field?" Philippa asked quietly.

Lee nodded. "I could never afford to buy a companion for him though," he added.

"I was thinking of Jubilee," went on Philippa. "I normally only keep her here in the winter, but I lost my grazing last week and I haven't been able to find anywhere else." "My field's three miles from here," Lee warned.

Philippa smiled. "I don't mind that as long as the grass is good and Jubilee is happy," she said.

Lee observed the contentment on Nugget's face, now that he had found a friend. "I am sure they will both be happy," he said.

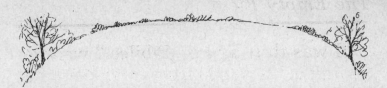

Catch as Catch Can

Tamsin had to get off her bicycle and push it up the last part of the lane. With a saddle across the handlebars and a bridle and grooming kit behind the seat, it was too heavy to pedal. Despite this, she hurried on with her heart racing with excitement as she looked forward to her first real ride on Cracker.

She had been on him before, at the Smith's when she was trying him out. However, that was not the same as having him to herself as her own pony to ride wherever she wanted to ride, without having to wait for the instructress to trot-on, or to ask his real owner if she could try him over a little jump.

Tamsin padlocked her bicycle to the fence, picked up the bridle and climbed into the field. Her pockets were full of carrot tops and breadcrusts. She'd wisely brought plenty, in case the other ponies came up when she called for Cracker.

Aladdin lifted his head and started up the hill before Cracker issued a neigh and came cantering up, punching bared teeth at the others to keep them off his feed.

During the last week, she had come up after school every day with an apple and a bag of pony cubes to feed him. Cracker guessed the same was in store this morning, until he saw the bridle on Tamsin's shoulder. Then, he skidded to a halt.

"Cracker! Come on, there's a good boy," cried Tamsin as she pulled the

Cracker skidded to a stop when he saw the bridle

slice of bread from her pocket and waved it at him. The pony tensed, he pulled his hindlegs under him and waited for Tamsin to approach. When she was close enough, he sprang forward, whipped the bread from her fingers and jumped aside to swing his quarters in her face.

"Cracker!" Tamsin ran in pursuit, but he broke into a canter, bucking, and did not stop and face her until she stopped running.

Tamsin bit her lip. "Cracker, let me catch you!" she pleaded. She took another slice of bread from her pocket and approached more cautiously. She did not like to admit it, but she was scared that he might kick her. "Come on, be a good boy," she coaxed him gently waving the slice of bread beneath the pony's nose. He sidled to keep out of reach, facing her but very much on guard.

Carefully, he watched Tamsin, judged his moment and poked forward to grasp the bread and spin round in a

single movement. "Cracker, stop it!" she cried out. This was hopeless. Tamsin struck her leg with the reins and stared after the pony, her eyes pricking with tears. There was only one slice of bread remaining.

This time, she kept the bait closer to her side so that Cracker had to come nearer to reach it. "Come on, come on," Tamsin coaxed and Cracker pushed his neck forward until the bread was tantilizingly close.

Tamsin slowly raised her left hand.

Her fingers reached for the pony's mane. Cracker took one step and as he snatched the bread, Tamsin grasped his mane. Cracker spun aside, pulling her off balance and Tamsin fell, dragging a tuft of hair from Cracker's mane as she wrenched her fingers loose.

She cried. She could not help it. Cracker was hightailing it to the bottom of the field, whinnying his victory to the other ponies. She would never catch him now.

Her own pony, running away from her! She had never imagined it would be like this. Tamsin pushed herself to her feet, stuffed the bridle into her bicycle bag and unfastened the padlock. All that effort for nothing. She hated Cracker.

At that moment, she was filled with loathing for him. It had been more fun going to the riding school. At least there, the ponies nuzzled her. They didn't turn away or knock her over. Also, at the riding school, she had not

Catch as Catch Can

Tamsin watched her pony hightailing it to the bottom of the field

had to catch a pony. She had simply paid her money and gone into the yard where a pony would be tied up waiting for her, already groomed and saddled. Tamsin threw her leg over the bar and pedalled slowly home. She would not give in to Cracker. She would go back tomorrow. Soon, he would miss his feeds and he would come to her.

At eleven o'clock on Sunday morning, Tamsin's fingers closed on thin air. All she had for her effort was a straggle of wiry mane as Cracker spun nimbly away from her. "You horrid pony!" she shouted angrily. "If you don't stop being so naughty I will never feed you again!" Cracker ignored her, trotting jauntily away with his tail high and snorting with self-satisfaction.

Tamsin sighed heavily, her disappointment turning her heart to lead. What did the pony care for her threats when he had all this grass to eat! "Are you having problems?" an eloquent voice asked.

Beyond the gate sat a girl on a pretty

dapple-grey pony. Tamsin frowned and then recognized her as Isobelle Dale, a girl who went to the private school in Chattam and won every showing class in the county with her registered Dartmoor mare. Isobelle Dale won everything and knew everything, at least that was what Tamsin had been led to believe by her school friends. She herself had not met the girl before.

"Haven't you got a halter?" Isobelle asked.

There you are, thought Tamsin, she's

trying to show off. Tamsin hoped the girl had not been watching long, for if she had the sight of her spending an hour trying to catch Cracker was enough to make her a laughing stock.

"You would find it much easier," Isobelle went on. The grey mare lifted her head and whinneyed to Cracker. "He might come closer now that Seaspray is here. Move slowly and keep calm and try again."

Tamsin turned away. She had a good mind to tell Isobelle to mind her own business, but Cracker wanted to make friends with Seaspray and that provided an opportunity to catch him which she just could not resist. She moved closer to the gate and waited quietly. When Cracker came close enough, she caught tight hold of his neck. He pulled away, but did not run off as he had before.

"You will find a rope halter is much easier than a bridle because you don't have to get the bit in and with the loose rein you can slip it over his neck without him seeing." Isobelle explained. "I used to have the same trouble with Seaspray the first summer I had her. I was practising for so many shows she got bored and refused to be caught." She smiled and stroked her mare's neck. "You don't mean to do it, but it is so easy to forget that they have minds and hearts ... and they don't always like what we do."

Tamsin nodded. She felt guilty. Certainly, Cracker was being naughty in avoiding being caught, but she had never stopped to wonder why, had she? After all, he did not know that she meant him no harm. So far she was really a stranger to him. She patted his neck reassuringly. "You will get to like me, Cracker." she whispered. "You'll see – we shall go on lots of exciting rides together."

She tightened the girth, following Isobelle's instructions to pull up one of Cracker's forelegs to stretch the skin on his chest and smooth it free of wrinkles where the girth might rub. Then, she mounted, letting her legs fall neatly against Cracker's sides. Her hands felt just right on the reins. They rode up the land at a walk and, once through the gate into the woods, they stopped.

"You had better tighten Cracker's girth," advised Isobelle. "They nearly all hold their breath to make it slack when you saddle up."

Tamsin swung one leg forward and leaned over to pull the straps. Sure enough, the girth came up two holes on

Catch as Catch Can

Tamsin realized her hands felt just right on the reins!

each strap.

"Thank you for helping me out," she smiled at Isobelle. "I've only just got him and there's a lot to learn."

"It never never changes," grinned Isobelle. "Ponies are full of tricks. Do you feel up to a canter?"

Tamsin nodded enthusiastically and away they went, the ponies racing one another to the top of the bank, trees and grass flashing by. Tamsin felt blood pounding in her veins. This, she thought, was what she could never have enjoyed at the riding school, and she knew it had all been worth waiting for despite all the difficulties.

Rustlers
on the Moor

Rosalyn Walters shook two wads of straw onto Domino's bed and tossed the stalks loose with a pitchfork before banking up the sides of the bed against the stable walls like a huge nest. The piebald pony chewed at the rein of his lead rope and stuck his head through the bars to nudge Rosalyn's shoulder. "Just be patient," she responded, turning the straw in the centre to make a springy bed that would be warm to lie on and drain well to keep him dry.

Domino did not have a proper stable, if you think of loose-boxes as individual affairs with half doors that open onto a yard. His was a wooden-sided pen in one corner of the hay shed. He could not look out onto the world. That did have compensations, like now when it was dark and raining and Rosalyn was able to tie him outside the stable area and get on with bedding him down, without having him stirring the straw up with his feet.

Domino nudged her again and caught the shoulder of her jacket between his teeth. "I know, I know, you want your hay. Well, you will just have to wait," she told him and tossed the last forkful before tidying the front of the bed and pulling the release knot loose to lead him into the box.

"As if I would forget something for you!" She patted his neck. Domino was not merely a pony to Rosalyn, he was her friend. Despite living on a farm, her parents had not been keen to accept her interest in ponies. They were expensive and demanding pets, her father had said. Farms to him revolved around sheep and tractors.

Rosalyn had taken her pleas for a pony to her mother instead and made the point that her nearest friend was three miles away, four miles if she cycled to her along the roads.

Domino pawed the ground, demanding Rosalyn give her attention. "Okay, okay!" she said and scrambled to the top of the stack of bales to fill his haynet.

The barn door slid open and Rosalyn's father came in. "How much are you putting in there?" he called out. "Two wads for the night net," she told him and he nodded in a grumbly kind of way. "Remember it has got to last until March and there's my sheep going to be needing some soon," he reminded her.

Rosalyn slowed, trying to ignore Domino's whinny that she should hurry. Instead of going back to the house, her father was resting against the loose-box sides. "You're over-bedding him," he told Rosalyn. "Half that straw would have done."

"He makes holes and knocks himself on the floor with less," she explained.

"Then deep-litter him," suggested her father.

"His feet will crack," she replied.

"Not if you pick them out regularly," insisted her father, who was having the last word as usual.

Rosalyn bit her tongue on the follow-up that thin beds were a false economy.

She tried to ignore Domino's impatient whinny

Her father let the sheep run their straw into mush when they were brought off the moor. He would not understand that a horse had different needs.

When he had gone, she returned to the stable, swinging the net high against the fence before tying it securely. "Don't you worry, Domino, I'll see you don't go short," she told him. "I'll use the money I get at Christmas to buy in more straw and hay for you." She knew that would be difficult. Her pocket money was already stretched to the limit buying hard feed and keeping Domino's feet in shape. Rosalyn sighed at the thought of what she had been going to spend her Christmas money on – front shoes, so that she could ride him further afield. Now, they would have to wait.

In the kitchen, Rosalyn's mother had just filled the teapot and was trying to fend off the attentions of a hungry tortoiseshell cat with her foot. "Put some food down for her will you, Ros," she said, as her daughter came in.

Days were always busy at the farm. Christmas was the busiest with the snow to think of, all the extra shopping and family visits to fit in.

This year was more hectic than ever, since the rustlers had come into the dale. "Took ten head of Herefords from Grant's last night," Mr. Walters said as he stirred his tea. "I just hope they stick to cattle. I can't afford to lose any more sheep this year."

While her parents talked about the sheep, Rosalyn's thoughts were on her pony. After all, she thought, the sheep were free, and could always run away from rustlers. If the thieves ever got into the stable they would have no trouble getting Domino. So, as soon as she had finished eating, Rosalyn went out to the barn to check the doors were bolted. "If you hear any strangers, you call to me!" she told her pony before leaving him for the night.

There were no more raids for a couple of days. Mr. Walters thought the rustlers must have felt they'd had a narrow escape and moved on .The following Wednesday, Rosalyn emptied her schoolbag onto the bed only to discover she had left her geography textbook in her desk. The essay had to be handed in on Thursday morning and Miss Chambers was not one to accept excuses. She decided she had better ride over and borrow Judith's book.

"It's nearly dark," Rosalyn's mother pointed out when the riding hat appeared from the cupboard. "I

must go," explained Rosalyn. "Domino knows the way and I will stick to bridleways, so don't worry."

There was still a bit of light left in the day. Rosalyn turned her pony into the big fields that led down to the Kirby road. She put him into a steady canter, leaning forward with her arms down by his neck. There was a low hedge between the fields. They had jumped it a hundred times. Domino approached with his ears pricked and popped lightly over it. There was just enough light to take the road to the village. Rosalyn kept Domino to the verge and trotted along at a spanking pace.

Judith brought her own pony, Paladin, out into the yard when she saw Domino. "You've had him clipped!" Rosalyn exclaimed.

"My parents bought me a rug as an early Christmas present for him so I asked Tina to take off his extra woollies," explained Judith. She ran her hand down the clipping line along Paladin's throat and said: "I'll be able to go to horse trials and hunting. Winter riding will be interesting for a change. Any chance of having Domino done, then we can go out together?"

Rosalyn shook her head. She was having difficulty enough keeping Domino in shoes, without thinking of such extravagances as clipping. She gave a little sigh under her breath as she thought of the remarks her father would make – he'd probably call Domino a poodle!

"We could go together," Judith said

As usual, she stayed too long at Judith's but, she told herself, once it was dark it was dark. She phoned her parents to say she was on her way and took Domino along slowly by the longer route, since that bridleway was broad and easy going as well as being away from the road. The lane led them to a drove road on the moor that was marked in places with gravel and flat stones. Rosalyn put her hands in her pockets, leaving the reins loose on Domino's shoulder as he picked his own way.

She would not have noticed the lights if Domino had not put up his head, with his ears pricked and nostrils quivering as he trotted off the track. Her hands took up the reins to stop him and she peered into the darkness. Two spots of light moved, swaying up and down and then moving apart. There was a flash of movement near the ground and faintly the bleating of sheep from the valley.

Rustlers!

Rosalyn sat bolt upright in the saddle. Her first instinct was to gallop down and scatter the flock, but there were treacherous bogs between her and the other side of the valley. At speed in the darkness, they would be impossible to avoid.

There must be a truck. She screwed up her eyes trying to work out where the rustlers were heading. Then she remembered about Dean's Plantation. If the truck was parked on the far side it would not be seen from the road.

Rosalyn spun her pony round and galloped along the roadside verge, until Domino stumbled and almost threw her. "All right!" she whispered. "We'd better trot." It was hard to be cautious though, when she knew her father's sheep were being stolen.

Where the road curved round slowly, Rosalyn dropped to a walk and leaned out of the saddle until she could see the rough track across to the plantation. The men were close now and she could hear the sheep clearly. There was a scraping noise and a banging as the ramp of the truck went up. Rosalyn clapped her heels to Domino's sides, skimming round the back of the plantation as the men were climbing into the truck's cab.

"Steady now," she whispered. Letting the reins slack, she brought Domino up close to the truck and stood on her stirrups to reach for the tail bolts. Her hands closed on the rod of cold metal and pulled it loose as the truck's engine started. Exhaust fumes blew between

Domino's legs and sent him jumping to one side with a shrill neigh. Rosalyn caught up the rein. She heard the cab door open and sweat broke across her brow.

M588X

"Did you hear that, Bert?" said a gruff voice.

"Probably just the sheep," came someone's reply. "Come on, let's get away." Unfortunately, the first man was sure he had heard something odd and the cab door creaked wider.

Rosalyn lunged for the bolt, caught it

with the side of her hand and jerked it free. The ramp fell down and pandemonium broke loose. Domino leapt to one side. Rosalyn was thrown half out of the saddle and clutched her pony's neck as a dog leapt out of the cab and chased them over the heather.

The sheep bolted and broke the tailgates loose. Another dog set off after the sheep, but only served to scatter them as the men jumped out of the truck shouting and fuming.

Rosalyn pulled herself into the saddle and slapped her heels to the piebald's sides. The rough track led down to the farm and now that the moon was up she could follow it easily by the white stones that marked tyre tracks. Domino flew across the ground, never faltering. When they came to a gate at full speed, Rosalyn shut her eyes and prayed. Up into the air they flew and over, to speed on across the fields and into the yard. Floss and Beck ran out on their chains, yapping and leaping with excitement and the

Rosalyn shut her eyes and prayed as the sheep scattered

kitchen door opened.

"Rustlers!" Rosalyn called out. "On the moor – I managed to get the sheep out!"

Her father pushed out, shouting: "Where are they, Ros?"

"Dean's Plantation," she cried.

"Call the police and get Danny Glover up there to help me, Eileen," Mr. Walters told his wife as he was picking up the Land-Rover keys and slipping the chains from the dogs.

Suddenly the yard was empty. Rosalyn jumped down and stroked Domino's neck. He was hot and sticky with sweat. She would have to cool him before he was turned into the stable. She ran the stirrups up on their leathers and loosened the girth. Then she led him into the nearby field and plodded slowly round. After two circuits his breathing had settled and she brought him back onto the hard ground of the yard.

Domino winced and his head nodded unevenly. Rosalyn felt her heart turn over. She took the reins over his head and trotted him out. The limp was more noticeable, every time his near foreleg touched the ground.

"Oh dear, what have you done?" she said. Back in the stable, Rosalyn picked up his feet and found them pocked with gravel. The off fore had a sharp stone wedged in the groove between the frog and the sole. She managed to prise it out, but the sole beneath had been badly bruised. "Poor Domino, you will have a good bed tonight and a long rest to ease that," she assured the pony.

It was much later when Rosalyn's father came back. "Did you catch them?" she asked anxiously when he came through the door. "Yes, we got them, but not until after they'd led us a dance all over the moor first!" he said, clapping Rosalyn's shoulders. "You did a good job there, lass," he added.

"It's Domino you should thank," Rosalyn told him. "I rode him so fast, he's lame!"

Mr. Walters was silent a moment and

then he smiled: "See he has a good bed down and once his feet are better I'll get the blacksmith up to put some shoes on him."

"Oh, thanks Dad!" cried Rosalyn and she ran from the room to tell Domino his good fortune. He blinked, surprised to see her but he livened up at the smell of a carrot taken from the vegetable rack. Rosalyn laughed as she stroked his neck.

"Now that you have saved Dad's sheep he'll never say a bad word against you," she laughed. "Who knows, I might see you clipped yet!"

Count Your Blessings

The bus passed the sign for Bishopton and hawthorn hedges gave way to terraced rows. I fastened the buttons of my jacket and slipped the book I had been reading into a side pocket of my bag. Soon, I would see Slipstep, Imogen's pony. When we started writing to each other six months ago she had been, like myself, pony-mad but pony-less.

Then her birthday had come along and she was given a pony. I'd tried to persuade my parents to do the same thing for me, but they had refused. We lived in a city, so I had to put up with once a week at the riding school instead. How envious I was of Imogen!

Slipstep was a beautiful pony. Imogen had sent me lots of photographs of her grazing in the field, or standing waiting for a ride. She stood twelve-one hands high. Her head was fine, and veins almost visible across her cheeks as they ran into soft round nostrils. Her ears were small and sprouted tufts of silvery hair. Her eyes were large and dark.

Imogen said she went like the wind. I couldn't wait to try her. Most of my lessons took place in a covered school with Mrs. Williams, or her instructress, standing in the middle shouting at us to sit deeper and keep our lower legs back. They were great believers in riding without stirrups to develop balance and in exercises in the saddle. I could touch my toes at a trot but I had never galloped in my life.

The bus pulled into a cobbled square

and in no time at all I was in the car
with Imogen and her mother, sweeping
along country lanes to the tiny village
of Crawthorne Gill. Imogen lived in the
end house of a stone terrace. Slipstep
was stabled at the farm next door and
we went round immediately to see him.
When Imogen said *farm* I had thought
of something like the riding stable only
with cattle instead of horses. Valley
View Farm was very different. The
doors hung from their hinges, the
gutters sprouted grass and the yard

had never seen concrete. Imogen ploughed on as if she hadn't seen the mud, while I hovered at the gate and tip-toed from tussock to tussock trying to keep the sticky dirt off my shoes.

"Watch where you put your hands," Imogen said when I reached the stable and she pointed to the chickens on the rafters.

Slipstep put her head over the door, whickered and nodded. I went over to her and lifted my hand to stroke her nose, but she tried to nip me.

Imogen laughed when she saw me jerk my hand away and said: "She is just being friendly, Kate – watch!" She pulled off her glove and put her hand under Slipstep's nose. The pony nuzzled it and then began to lick with long, rhythmic strokes. "They are supposed to like the salt or something," Imogen said. "Just make sure you always hold your palm flat and keep your fingers together."

I nodded, feeling rather embarrassed. Imogen would think I knew nothing,

Count Your Blessings

Imogen warned me to go carefully as I followed her to the stable

but then I didn't as far as being with ponies was concerned. At Mrs. William's stable, the horses were always tacked up ready for the ride and you were lucky if you got to lead them from their boxes.

"Do you want to help me bed her down?" Imogen asked.

"Aren't we going to ride?" I tentatively suggested.

"There isn't enough time," replied Imogen quickly.

"It's only four o'clock, it won't be dark for ages yet," I persisted.

"It's too late," Imogen stated brusquely. She turned her back on me and started scooping pony cubes into a bucket. "There's some hay soaking in the barrel outside – go and get it will you, Kate."

Her voice seemed tight, as if she was hiding something. But what? In her letter, Imogen had promised that I could ride with her every day. Maybe she had changed her mind. I must seem like an idiot to her. With all the stories I had told about things we learned in our lessons, she probably expected someone better.

I took hold of the haynet and heaved. I would have to show Imogen that I wasn't just a city girl and I could help out with all the jobs. The net came up and dirty brown water slopped over the lip and splashed my jeans. Although I stopped to let the net drain, it still soaked me. There was just no way I could carry the horrid thing without it banging against my legs This was something I would not miss when I went back to Mrs. Williams!

The next morning dawned beautifully fine. Surely we would ride today! Hoping we would, I pulled on my jodhpurs and took my riding boots out of the plastic bag I had packed them in and found my riding hat and string gloves. Mrs. Williams was a stickler for dress if you rode there often. She went on and on about the right clothes helping you sit correctly, because they were designed for that purpose.

Imogen, however, was wearing jeans and a sweater.My heart dropped like a stone. "You'd better put on something else," she advised. "There's the mucking out and grooming to do before we go out."

These jobs took an age and when we were finished, Imogen decided to put Slipstep back in the stable and go back to the house. "We might as well go out after lunch now," she said.

Finally, we were saddling up. My heart raced with excitement and when

Imogen asked if I would like to ride first I did not hesitate. Slippy was a small pony by comparison to the ones I had ridden at the stables, so I had no trouble mounting. By the time I got the stirrups down to the right length, I felt very comfortable on the broad-seated old saddle.

I gathered up the reins ready for action, touched my heels to Slipstep's sides and kicked her gently as she plodded after Imogen. My dreams of galloping over the moor vanished. It took all my efforts to make Slippy break into a trot. Also, we went a long way without Imogen suggesting that we should swop and I wondered if she felt guilty for not letting me ride the day before.

About a mile out of the village there was a wide verge. "Can I have a try at a canter?" I asked.

"If you want to," Imogen replied.

Slipstep must have sensed my decision. Before I had gathered the reins she had ducked her head down, taken hold of the bit and spun round. The next thing I knew I was hanging on her mane as she galloped flat out down the road. I managed to pull myself back into the saddle and tried hard to slow her, but her mouth was set and with a bank ahead of us I shut my eyes and clung on for dear life.

Slipstep skidded round a corner into the High Street, streaked past the farm and stopped suddenly outside her field gate. Her head went up as she put on the brakes and I flew up her neck to

meet it, but I managed to stay on.

My breath came in short, sharp gasps. My legs trembled against the saddle. If I had fallen off at that speed ... if she had slipped over...

Slipstep put her head over the field gate making it clear that she wanted the ride over and to get on with grazing. This must have sparked off some hidden resource of courage in me, because I jumped down onto my unsteady legs and ran up the stirrups. I took the reins over her head and turned her back towards the village. When I tried to lead her, Slippy dug in her heels and shook her head.

"Oh, yes you will!" I commanded, raising a hand to threaten her. I smacked her rump and she jumped forward. The next time she stopped I only had to raise my voice to get her moving.

We met Imogen at the bank. Her cheeks were red from running and her eyes swollen with unshed tears. "Are you all right?" she squeaked. I nodded. "I'm sorry Imogen, but I couldn't stop her," I panted.

"It's my fault," explained Imogen. "I should have warned you, but she's never been that bad before. Usually, she only pulls when you have actually turned for home." Imogen began to cry. "You could have been killed," she sobbed. "It would have been my fault if you had."

"What do you mean?" I asked.

"Well, she was all right when she came," went on Imogen, "but then she

We met Imogen at the bank. She was running towards us

started playing me up, like she did today. She would only go quickly on the way home. I couldn't make her canter away from home so I always saved them for when we turned round. Then I couldn't stop her and I got scared – she's so strong!"

Imogen bit her lip. "I hardly dare ride her these days," she confessed. I put my arm around my friend's shoulders. "We'll get her sorted out", I reassured her, "you'll see and we can start now. Up you get!" I started to pull down the stirrups.

"No! I couldn't!" exclaimed Imogen, looking horrified.

"I'll lead her if she starts anything," I promised.

"All right then," Imogen finally agreed. She mounted and held the saddle tightly with her hands. "We could try a drop noseband and a martingale on her to start with," I suggested. "They would make her easier to control until she learns to behave herself."

"If you think so," agreed Imogen. "We will go into the town tomorrow. There's a saddler in the market square."

When we got back, we turned Slippy into the field and went indoors to clean her tack and discuss our plans to reform her. I was sure we could get the pony sorted out if we worked together. It meant never letting her go faster than a walk on the way home and making her trot and (if we were lucky enough!) canter on the out.

All it needed was time, as well as

strength as I discovered when I woke up the next morning, aching in muscles I didn't know existed. Imogen's mother laughed when she saw us hobbling down the stairs, but that did not stop us going out to begin our training programme for Slippy.

It was hardly a miracle, but by the time I left Imogen had overcome her fear and Slipstep was stoppable when she got excited. We also found we could anticipate when she was going to turn and that helped a lot.

Saturday came all too quickly and I was boarding the bus to take me home and waving goodbye to Imogen. All that lay ahead of me now was one lesson a week until the summer, when Imogen had promised to invite me over to stay again.

Mrs. Williams's stables ... I sighed and leaned my head against the glass, but I didn't feel sad. I had more a feeling of quiet anticipation, because handling Slippy had made my lessons seem worthwhile and I knew that the future would make me appreciate them even more. In fact, I was looking forward to them. Maybe I did not have my own pony, but I did have a good teacher.

I smiled to myself because my grandmother would be proud to hear me count my blessings!

The Lie

The grey's stride was long and silky. When I asked him to canter, he barely increased his speed but rocked off his hindlegs with his head held high, and his neck nicely arched. It was an easy stride to follow, so different from the jostling gaits of the riding school ponies who stuck their heads down and shook your bones loose.

Excalibur's pricked ears and his steady movements were a perfect example of alertness and obedience. His stable manners, Emma Stephenson had assured me, were faultless. I was inclined to believe her, having noticed that Excalibur did not nip when the girths were tightened, or sidle when I turned the stirrup to mount.

I longed to make the canter we were having last for ever, but alas we were soon back at the gate. I was drawing him to a walk and then asking him to stand squarely and backrein a few paces. Mrs. Stephenson smiled at me, thinking she had a sale on her hands. Her daughter Emma stroked the grey's neck. "He has been placed in a couple of dressage competitions, but I've only just started schooling him seriously for them," she said.

"I can see why he has done so well," I said enthusiastically. "His paces are very smooth and balanced."

"Excalibur is really a jumping horse," Mrs. Stephenson gave me a reminder. "Grade C standard – he is very fast. Emma, put up some jumps to try him over. Are you all right at that height or should we lower them first?"

I cast a glance at the professional looking jumps with their striped poles and glossy wings. They were bigger than anything I had jumped before, but then Excalibur was bigger too.

"They'll be fine ," I replied in a tone I hoped gave the impression I jumped this height every day. I shortened my stirrups, put Excalibur into a collected canter and turned to the first jump which was a spreading triple bar.

He took a strong hold on the bit and leapt away at it. "Steady!" I whispered, my hands tightening on the reins and checking him gently. One, two, three strides and he took off and cleared the jump in a lazy arc. Patting him my thanks, I let him return to the gate on a loose rein.

Emma was biting her fingernails. She stroked Excalibur's neck when we stopped.

"You can see why I want a competitive home for him," explained Mrs. Stephenson.

"Certainly," I agreed, "it would be a

waste not to. I'll have to check with my father before I can say *yes* for certain. He likes me to try the ponies on my own first and only comes out to see any I really like."

"He sounds like a busy man," smiled Mrs. Stephenson.

"He is," I assured her. "I'll call you this evening."

"Will you be keeping the horse at home?" enquired Emma and I told her of the stable in the paddock behind the bungalow, Emma nodded and said

Excalibur would like that. "He enjoys being around people," she said.

"Paddock and stable," I repeated to myself later as I walked up the pavement to our terrace house, shaking my head. The nearest we came to a field, let alone a paddock, was the patch of grass that cut us off from the road and my mother's flower-pots in the backyard.

"Take your boots off as you come in, Trudy!" Mum called out when she heard the front door open. She was in the living room, ironing shirts in between talking to our neighbour Mrs. Trent. My sister Liza had her cassette player on so loud I could hardly hear myself think. She wouldn't turn it off (I knew that from experience) so I took refuge in the bathroom which was the one place in the house you could lock the door on intruders.

I washed, changed into clean jeans and a tee-shirt and then sat down heavily on the laundry basket, feeling sorry for myself.

Paddocks and stable!

Who was I kidding? When I started this make-believe game, the lies I told didn't affect me. I knew very well I could not buy the horses I was trying out, but gradually things had changed. I had never meant to lie, not in a really bad way – it was just that I wanted a horse to ride.

You see, I had been going for riding lessons once a week for the last three years and learned about as much as I could hope to from Mrs. Mullins and her ponies. During that time I had saved two hundred pounds towards a pony of my own. My parents had promised to put something towards the price and cost of stabling, but even so it was not nearly enough for the sort of animal I wanted.

When I started looking, I did stay within my price range, but all the ponies were hopeless. They were either unbroken two-year-olds, or so small it was embarrassing to get on them. I wanted a decent pony, around fourteen-two hands with a good jump and nice to look at.

By chance, the people I visited one day had their pony up for sale. "Lori will suit you nicely," the owner had said. In no time at all, I was in the saddle and trying out a classy pony for the first time in my life. Then the idea I came up with was very simple. All I had to do was telephone any seller and make an appointment to try their pony out, only to discover sadly it was not quite right for me. I shrugged and stood up. I wasn't going to start feeling

The idea was simple for all I had to do was to telephone the seller of a pony

guilty about it now. There was no harm done and the whole idea had given me a chance to sit on something with quality for a change, like Excalibur.

Two weeks later I took the bus to Stapely and got off at the foot of Ox Pasture lane on yet another of my expeditions. At the end of the lane, there was a low stone farmhouse with hens pecking weeds in the yard and washing flapping in the garden. A boy of about eighteen came out of the back door and waved to me. "Trudy Bell?" he called out. I nodded and he waved me over to one of the barns.

I swear that when I clapped my eyes on Foxtrot, my heart actually stopped beating. She was stunning. A chestnut mare with a fine face and long, silky-smooth Arabian mane. She put her head over the door, whickering to James Rowe through soft nostrils, her big dark eyes full of intelligence and understanding.

"Part-bred Arab," said James, opening the door and slipping in with the bridle. "She is registered, I have papers indoors." He ran his hand up the mare's neck. Foxtrot tossed her head away, showing the white of her eye. "She's still a bit head-shy," explained James. You have to be gentle with her when you bridle because I think she had been knocked about a bit when I got her. She's a good ride, mind – she just needs a sympathetic rider."

I nodded, unable to take my eyes off the mare. He could have told me she bucked like a mule and I'd still have wanted to try her.

Foxtrot swept over the ground with that wonderful, floating Arabian movement. I didn't want to get off her. It wasn't so much that she was better schooled than the others because in some ways she was probably behind them. Although she was not quite so polished, her enthusiasm made up for this. We seemed to strike a chord in one another. I walked, trotted and cantered her and then let her go along one side of the field with a burst of gallop.

"She seems to like you," James Rowe said when I brought the mare back to the gate.

I smiled. "The feeling is mutual," I told him as I shook my feet from the stirrups and jumped down. "I'll have to speak to my parents, but I can tell you now I like her very much."

I liked Foxtrot so much I got off the bus three stops early and called at Grange Farm to ask Mr. Slade if he still had grazing spare. The fact that Foxtrot cost four times as much as I had to spend was not something I was prepared to dwell on. At least not until I got into the narrow streets that smelled of exhaust fumes and heard my mother shouting to me to take my boots off as I came in.

I remembered the houses I had been to with whips and riding hats in the hall, with china horses on the mantle and *Horse and Hound* or *Riding* on the coffee table or a spaniel curled up in front of the hearth. In place of these country features all I saw at home was a pile of ironing, forgotten mugs of coffee and the newspaper open at the football page. A prickling sensation took possession of me. It was despair. My chest felt tight and my eyes burned. I dashed for the bathroom, slammed the bolt home and collapsed on the floor, my hand in my mouth as I cried.

It was no good. Today, I had actually started believing the lies myself. I sniffed back the tears and blew my nose hard. Foxtrot had brought me up short because I wanted her so much. Now, I had to face the truth that I would never be in a position to buy her - never!

For three weeks I did not look at another horse. When Mum suggested a shopping trip to Harton, I went along with the plan of buying a pair of jeans or a skirt to wear at the end of term dance. However, we split up in town and I got lost amongst the back streets. When I heard a neigh quite close my feet took me sharp right and into a cattle market packed today with trailers,

A chestnut filly had just been led into the ring

saddlery and horses.

The stalls were filled with a mixed collection of hunters in soft condition, feathered piebalds, children's ponies with vets' certificates and potted histories stapled to their box doors, as well as a selection of young stock. A chestnut filly had just been led into the ring when I reached it. She was three years old, according to the catalogue, and lightly broken. Her face was pretty.

The steward lifted his hand to chivvy the filly along and she threw up her head in a gesture which reminded me of Foxtrot. I stood up abruptly and found myself bidding.

The price crept up, but it stayed within my limits and this was just as well for five minutes later I was down in the stables to collect what had become my horse! Chance, for that was the filly's name, ran away from me. "Hey, there!" I crooned. "Steady girl!"

I crossed the box slowly, whispering to her as one hand was held out to gently stroke her neck. Slowly, the white went out of her eyes and she turned her head to look at me more closely.

"That's more like it," I told her. "We are going to be friends, Chance, you and I. I have to go and sort out some transport for you and find my parents, but I'll be back soon."

Now that she had quietened, I put my arms about her neck and hugged her. All the fancy horses were forgotten and I did not miss them. Chance was my pony and at my level. We would learn together. Maybe one day she would be like Foxtrot, and if she was I would know it was my care that had got her there and not any stupid, silly stories that I had made up!

Coming Up Trumps

Michael brought back his right hand, drew it to the side a little and flexed his wrist. His left heel moved back to press Verity's ribs behind the girth to make her curve her spine as she turned. As so often of late, the mare resisted him, twitching her ears back and catching the bit between her teeth. "You are in a bad temper today," Michael quipped. "Come on, behave yourself - let's get this over with and then we can have a crack at the jumps."

He sat deeply in the saddle. His pelvis bounced as he tried to follow the mare's jolting trot. Verity was in no mood for easy riding. She swished her tail and stuck her head in the air, hollowing her back and making it difficult for him to maintain good contact with her.

Michael sighed and let her come to a walk. His mouth was grim. Flatwork was not his cup of tea at the best of times, but it had to be done. He had bought Verity because of her scopey jump and good track record in the ring, but experience alone was not enough to win at the county show. They had to work to develop the suppleness and obedience that would make her fast over a twisting course.

Michael pulled back on both reins and Verity came to a square halt. There were only three jumps in the paddock – an upright, a parallel and a hog's back, all of which could be jumped in two directions The route plotted in his mind, Michael pushed

Verity into a trot. Turning towards the hog's back he put his heels on to ask for a canter. Verity remained in trot. Michael dug his heels into her ribs and she spun out to the side, putting her head down and running for the gate.

"Oh, no you don't Madam! You are going to jump that fence even if it takes all evening !" Michael cried and pulled the bay mare round to drive her at the fence again, kicking hard. Verity took two strides and went up on her hindlegs. She did not rear very high, but her ears were back and she spun round sharply.

Michael's brow furrowed as he debated with himself what to do next. All horses tried out a few tricks on new owners to test their skill, but that generally happened in the first week. He had possessed Verity for three months now and at the outset she had jumped marvellously. He turned the mare one last time and she fought him every step of the way. A little shiver passed through Michael's shoulders.

Michael knew that horses do sometimes try out tricks on their owners

What if she was in pain? It couldn't be her tack because he had cleaned that earlier in the week and besides, she had always jumped with this saddle. But what if she had a spine weakness?

Michael's cheeks flushed. Verity might not have felt it when the jumps were low, but now that he was asking something of her, now that she needed to have scope, she would feel the pain. With a bitter sigh, Michael dismounted knowing he should never have tried to save money by skipping over the vet's certificate when he bought Verity. He had assumed that she must be fit. She had gone well in the paddock but she was an older horse and she had been out of practice a bit since her rider had gone ski-ing and broken her ankle.

He had thought he was getting a bargain in good condition. With more recent wins behind her, the mare would be worth well over a thousand pounds. However, if she had a spine weakness and was no longer fit to jump, he would be lucky if he could sell her for half the

price his father had paid out at Christmas.

Michael put Verity into her loose-box and crossed the farmyard. "What's up with you?" Lee Robertson called out. "Got thrown again?"

"I'm not like you, I stick to the saddle," Michael retorted. "No, it's not that. Verity's feeling out of sorts. I'll have to call the vet to her."

"You should have traded her in for a motorbike," laughed Lee.

Michael turned away. Two years ago, Lee had been interested in ponies and they had ridden together and raced each other in practice for the gymkhana games. When they outgrew their first ponies, Lee turned to motorcycles and now they grumbled at each other for messing up the tracks.

Mr. Hart arrived at Green Knoll Farm two hours later, by which time Verity had scoffed her haynet and was looking around for more. That was another thing, Michael thought to himself as he led Mr. Hart to the stable, she ate and ate. Although she was only one hand higher than his first pony, Kestrel, she ate nearly twice as much. All in all, she looked like she was turning into an expensive bargain.

"Playing up and won't jump, you say?" said the vet.

"That's right," Michael told him. "It's been getting slowly worse. I thought she was just trying it on with me at first, but it has got worse!"

"Your tack is in good condition?" enquired Mr. Hart and Michael told him the leather was soft and the tree firm.

"Hmmm!" Mr. Hart pulled Verity's eyelids back to look at the inner membrane. He felt the pulse in her neck, ran his hand along her spine and then got out a thermometer to take her temperature. As he moved her tail, he began to smile. "I've got an idea I know her problem," he said.

"Will she get better?" was Michael's anxious question.

"Oh, certainly," smiled Mr. Hart ."It is a passing condition – she's going to have a foal!"

"What!" Michael fell back against the door in surprise. "When?" he gasped.

Mr. Hart explained how Verity was already beginning to broaden and her hips starting to hollow.

"It could be as early as three weeks," he told Michael.

Michael wiped his brow, finding it difficult to keep up with what was happening. The county cup drifted out of reach – no wonder she wasn't able to jump. "Is the foal all right?" he asked, now full of concern.

"Seems to be," said Mr. Hart. "She's an old mare and has had several foals before – that made it harder to detect this one. She's fit and healthy. Turn her out to grass, or give her exercise on a lead rein and everything should be fine."

"I just had no idea," muttered an astonished Michael.

"Haven't you had her long?" Mr. Hart asked, packing up his things as Michael told him: "Just three months.

"I've got an idea I know her problem!" exclaimed the vet

She was sold to me as a working horse and I was training her for the summer."

"If she was warranted a working horse and not a brood mare you could try to send her back, but three months is a long time." The vet gave a crooked smile. "You will have the mare jumping again in the autumn and who knows, maybe you will have a future showjumper on your hands with the foal. Call me if you need any more advice."

"I will and thank you," stammered Michael. A future showjumper the foal might be, but surely then the owners would have known that and kept her? Unless they did not realize she was in foal ... Michael hung over the door to watch Verity make her way through another net of hay. Knowing his luck, the foal would be a feather-legged twelve-two pony.

As a mother-to-be, Verity would need good feed and plenty of it as well as vitamins to make sure she was strong enough to go into work again in the summer. That meant more expense. Also he would not be riding her from now on, not for several months.

Michael remembered the Saturday job on his uncle's vegetable stall.

Looked like he would be taking it up after all. Verity pulled a mouthful of hay out of the net and wandered over to lip Michael's sleeve. He stroked her neck and knew then that he could not sell her. As Mr. Hart had said, there would be shows at the end of summer and he would be able to jump her again then. They would get by, one way or another, they would get by . . .

Three weeks later, Michael was again leaning against the stable door. Verity crossed the floor to nudge him and then wandered back to her hay. She seemed in a temper with herself. Her ears laid back when she turned to her stomach and she could not settle, not even when he brought her feed.

Dark patches broke out on her brown neck. Slipping the bolt, Michael approached her, one hand held out. "Steady, there's a girl," he crooned. Verity swished her tail and shook her head then pushed her muzzle against him. Her coat was hot and sticky with sweat. The hollows above her flanks were now pronounced.

She wandered away from him, stirring the straw with restless hoofs. Michael bit hard on his lip. The vet had said her foaling should be easy, but if something had gone wrong he wouldn't recognize the danger until too late.

Verity could die!

The mare's knees buckled and she lay down with a heavy grunt. Michael's feet found wings as he sped to the farmhouse. His fingers slipped on the telephone dial and he stammered his call out so fast that the receptionist had to make him repeat it.

Michael hurried back across the yard, then made his feet slow to a walk because the receptionist had told him his worrying could possibly make the mare anxious.

Verity now lay flat out on the straw. "Verity!" Michael's cry brought her head up and he let out a sigh of relief. He made to open the door, but she laid back her ears and snapped at him before rolling onto her chest and looking behind her to the wet bundle by her hindlegs.

Michael felt a smile split his face. He watched in silence as Verity stood up and turned to lick her new-born foal. The tiny creature tried to move its head. Its ears flopped against its head. There was no strength in its neck and when it pushed itself onto its stomach it sat with its chin on the straw, breathing heavily.

A car came into the yard. Michael welcomed the vet, talking excitedly and by the time he returned to the stable the foal was trying to get up. The first time it managed two steps and then toppled sideways. Michael went to help it, but Mr. Hart held him back. On its second attempt the foal got to its mother's side.

"You've been lucky with this one, I'd say," Mr. Hart declared when he finished hs examination. "This little colt has the making of a fine horse."

"How big do you think he will grow?" Michael wanted to know.

"Feed him well and he could make sixteen hands," the vet told him. "That star is The Entertainer's mark if I'm not mistaken – nice ex-racehorse over by Barrowby. Where did you get the mare?"

Michael smiled. "Little Barrowby," he said.

"Looks like your gamble came off then," laughed Mr. Hart. "He'll make a handsome horse for you in four years' time. What will you call him?"

Michael looked at the dark brown foal, with its wobbly legs and big knees. He tried to imagine it as a four-year-old, standing taller than its mother and bursting with energy. The foal turned to peer at him through half focused eyes. The star was distinctive, a sharp diamond shape slap in the centre of his forehead.

"I think I'll call him Trumps," Michael said.

A Spectacular Pony

Quicksilver stretched his neck low and galloped flat out, his small round hoofs thundering upon the peat track. The wind brought tears to my eyes, yet I leaned forward and urged him faster, drumming at his ribs with my heels until the heather passed by us in one long dark blur.

Robert Laverne and Brenda were waiting on the ridge. Their faces were suitably impressed by Quicksilver's performance on the gallop. As I came into line with them I dug my knees into the saddle rolls and pulled back sharply. Quicksilver skidded to a halt.

"Wow, Norma! He can't half motor!" Brenda enthused. Her little bay pony, Easter, looked on with pricked ears. He considered galloping too much effort, preferring to keep to a steady plod.

Quicksilver jogged, bouncing about underneath me with his head high and the breeze lifting his lovely mane. He could be tiresome with his skittering about act, especially when he put on a performance in the showing ring. To be honest, though, I quite liked having him jumping out of his skin like this, all bursting with energy and full of the desire to gallop.

He reared frequently, but I only came off the first time because he took me by surprise. Now, I simply leaned forward. Sometimes I could get him to rear to command (sort of, anyway) like now, if I turned him away from home and dug in my heels.

I suppose it's not quite the right thing to do, but it was fun sometimes and he made quite a spectacle on his back legs. That was what I liked about him all along, he was a real *looker*.

There was Arabian blood in him somewhere, to judge from his fine-boned face. His colour was a lovely pale grey with black points like smudges at knees, hocks, feet and around his eyes and muzzle. His mane and tail were long and full and absolutely pure white. His action was flashy, especially his high-stepping trot. I liked that, as I'd wanted a pony with a bit of spirit to it and not some old Dobbin anyone could sit on.

We had reached the road now and

went into single file on the verge. Quicksilver pulled, trying to get his neck out straight which would make him impossible to control. "Oh, no you don't!" I muttered and tugged hard on the reins.

Quicksilver went up on his hindlegs, skittered sideways and then started to ping about on the tarmac. If the movements had been intentional, they might have been called dressage. Robert and the girls stopped, watching us with mixed expressions of horror and admiration. I pulled back my rein tightly after the third rear and then drove Quicksilver on at a spanking pace with the ponies cantering to keep up.

Brenda jogged alongside me as we came into the village. "I don't know how you dare ride him, Norma," she told me. "I wouldn't have the courage."

"It's not so difficult, so long as you have a really strong seat and don't let him panic you," I replied loftily.

She shook her head wonderingly and

said: "Rather you than me - see you tomorrow."

"At ten," I called after her. When the other ponies turned away, I let Quickie have his head and galloped up the narrow verge along the side of the road.

That evening, Dad collared me in the kitchen just as I was about to sneak out of the washing up. "Isn't it about time you had a new pony, Norma?" he said. I stopped abruptly. Could I believe my ears?

"You seem a bit long in the leg for Quicksilver these days," he added.

Guilt instantly made me wonder where he had seen me and if I had been doing anything wrong. I didn't think so as most of the fences we jumped were on and off the moor, well away from the village. "He is a bit small," I agreed, my sense of loss and disloyalty to Quickie considerably reduced by the thought of a nice fifteen-hand horse with plenty of substance and a scopey jump.

"Your birthday's coming up soon," Dad said. "It seems like a sensible time to start looking."

"It isn't that I don't like you," I told Quickie when I went out to feed him that night and straighten his New Zealand rug so that it no longer resembled a badly laid tablecloth, "but you are rather small for me now. I'll find you a good home, I promise."

So, I advertised and chewed away the best of my nails waiting for the telephone to ring. A week later, I had my first customer. She only gave me half-an-hour's notice, so I flew around like a mad thing to catch Quickie, slopping his tail into a bucket of water to whiten it and quickly brushing him over.

The girl was about eleven years old. She wore jodhpurs and long boots and had her hair in pigtails. Quickie turned to look at her, pricking his ears and whickering in an unusually friendly fashion. A shaft of sunlight broke through the clouds and lit him up dramatically.

I sensed that my luck was in!

Into the saddle I went and trotted Quicksilver round, keeping a tight rein. He seemed to be going quite well, so I sat down and asked for a canter. Off we went on a lovely collected stride. The little girl was almost falling over to get close to him. She patted his neck enthusiastically when we came to a halt.

"He's lovely," she smiled.

"He certainly has more about him than the other ponies we have seen," agreed her father.

"Can he jump?" the girl wanted to know.

"Like a stag," I told her confidently, because he could when he was in the mood. I turned him to face the permanent brush jump of woven hedge clippings and kicked him on. Quickie set his jaw and up he reared. The girl's mother and father gasped.

"He's not safe enough for Hannah!" announced the girl's father and the whole family trooped away.

Quickie set his jaw and up he reared

I jumped down grumpily. Not safe! What kind of pony *was* safe with a bit of quality in him? Anyway, Quickie was quite safe in the right hands. It wasn't his fault if the kid couldn't handle his class.

Ten more people came to see Quicksilver and all walked away the instant he reared. None of them shared the village children's view that rearing was exciting. I lost my temper with one family who started lecturing me about safety and told them they should go looking at seaside donkeys, because that was all they could handle.

Shortly before my birthday, Dad took me over to Eston to look at a horse he had heard about through the blacksmith. A superb animal, it was short-backed with a well muscled shoulder and good clean limbs. His stride felt incredibly slow and long after Quickie. His mouth was soft.

I was in love!

"I wish I didn't have to sell him," his owner confided to us, "but I have been

posted abroad. I want him to go to a good home and I must sell him quickly."

Dad nodded and explained: "We would be very keen to have him, but we must sell our own first. I'll get back to you on him as soon as I can."

"Do we really have to wait until Quicksilver is sold?" I asked Dad as we drove home.

"I'm not keeping two, Norma, I told you that," was Dad's abrupt reply.

"It's not my fault Quicksilver won't sell," I moaned.

"Whose fault is it then?" snapped Dad. "He's a good looking pony and he's fit. I want to see you ride him myself when we get back."

I suppose the mood I was in when I went out to saddle up didn't help. Anyway, to cut a long story short, Quickie was soon bored with showing off his paces in the field and shot off round it like a train. "You monster!" I shouted at him and tugged on the reins. Up he went on his back legs and then came down, snorting and dancing about.

"It's no wonder they won't buy him," choked Dad. "How long's he been doing this, Norma?"

"He always has done," I confessed.

"Well if you want Applause, you had better stop him right away," ordered Dad.

I stared after my father. I was struck dumb! Stop him rearing? How was I going to do that in an afternoon?

Furious with him, I spun Quickie round and took off up the field at full gallop, hurdling the fence onto the moor. We must have galloped five miles before I pulled up and by then Quickie was sweating and lathered. He put his head down to draw great gasping breaths.

Suddenly, I saw Quickie differently. I saw him as a brave little pony who was a bit full of himself maybe, but only a little pony indeed and one that I was getting too big and demanding for.

I bit my lip, seeing the obvious. Quicksilver, we hoped, would be bought for a child who probably had never owned a pony before. What parent would buy a pony that reared? I gave Quickie a long rein to walk home on. I had my work cut out, but I vowed I would school him properly from now on - not just so I could sell him and get Applause, but because I owed it to him that he should go on to enjoy a happy life.

His future was in my hands.

Circus Tricks

"Steady, Raven! Now you be good for me like you were yesterday and just keep walking." Lorna Eden gathered the webbing reins into her right hand and shifted backwards until she was sitting on the black gelding's rump. Raven kept up a steady walk but was unsure about just what was happening and he watched her from the corner of his eye.

Lorna had tried standing upright yesterday and failed because the horse's coat was too slippery. Today, she had put on trainers with grooved treads along the soles to see if they would help. She drew her legs up now and planted one foot squarely on Raven's broad rump.

The next bit was the hardest. Lorna's teeth bit into her lip. She counted the paces and then stretched upwards. Her left arm stuck out to help maintain balance and then she was standing, holding the reins at arm's length, with her knees flexed to take up the movement of each stride.

As Raven came round the bottom corner of the field Lorna caught sight of a familiar red car swinging into the drive. Her father was home early! She gulped, lost her balance and fell forward, her instincts pulling her legs under her so that she landed on her feet and still holding the reins.

The car stopped. "I thought I'd told you not to practise circus tricks on the horses!" Lorna's father shouted across the field.

"It doesn't hurt them," Lorna argued.

At last! Lorna found she was balancing on Raven's broad rump

"You'll mess up their training," snapped Mr. Eden. "A driving horse has to have a perfect mouth."

He got back into the car and drove to the house.

Lorna took her time following to make sure he would be indoors by the time she reached the yard. She had been practising with Raven for weeks now, using the half-hour she had before her parents got home from work to pursue her desire to be a circus rider. It would have to stop now because her father would soon be able to tell if she had been riding – he might even get her brother, Adam, to spy on her.

Like any other family on the night before a show, the Edens were outside until evening dusk, grooming the horses and polishing leather for the morning. Unlike the other families in the valley, their horses were identical – four blacks standing at fifteen hands high and not a white hair between them. Their tack was a driving harness with padded collars, broad traces and

supple crupper straps, all of soft dark leather with bright brass buckles.

Lorna's father had been driving ponies since he was old enough to sit in a trotting cart, but that had always been singles. This current passion for four-in-hand was only eight years old. Tomorrow's show would be a special one for him, being the first time he had entered a foursome made up entirely of horses he had bred himself.

It took two trucks to get the family and their equipment to the show ground. Lorna travelled in the transporter with her father and the four horses. Mrs. Eden followed in an ancient flat lorry with the cart chained down and covered in tarpaulin. She had Adam beside her as navigator.

Lorna tried to sleep, but was too excited. Her thoughts were full of the horses, especially Cinders. The young mare would be working with the eldest, Eclipse, and the two geldings Raven and Jet would be pulling behind.

Her father used to say they worked as a team already, because they were brothers and sisters. That should give him an advantage, but would it be enough, remembering that Cinders was only four years old?

Lorna jolted, banging her head against the window trim and realized she had fallen asleep. The horse-box had turned off the road and was bumping over a large field.

"Right then, let's get down to business!" Mr. Eden rubbed his hands enthusiastically and directed Adam

and Lorna to unbox the horses while he
and his wife eased the carriage down.

It wasn't really much of a carriage,
Lorna thought, glancing at the four-
wheel brake. Not like those you saw in
old coaching prints with gleaming
paintwork and brass coaching lamps.
Her brother used to call it a go-cart and
the name suited.

It was low and squat, narrow enough
to slip between the hazard posts but
wide enough for it not to topple at the
slightest corner. The wheels were made

of strengthened steel. It was built to withstand knocks and bumps and being dragged on its side by bolting horses.

Lorna brushed out Raven's tail and finished his coat with the soft stable rubber and a duster that laid his coat smoothly, and picked up the last specks of dust so that he gleamed like polished ebony.

Lorna's mother called the family over to take a break and a cup of coffee. Afterwards, they changed work clothes for their presentation outfits. These comprised of black jackets, jodhpurs and boots for Lorna and Adam. There was a tailored jacket for their father, along with driving apron and string gloves. A smart suit for their mother was finished off with a fine veil.

Mr. Eden took up the reins and set the team walking towards the arena. "Everybody ready?" he quipped. "Smile for the judge!" And they were in the ring.

There were twelve entries in the

Everybody changed into their presentation outfits

class. Each one was inspected by three judges to ensure the horses were clean, the carriage in good order and the whole appearance of the team workmanlike and attractive. Each driver then rode his test piece, following a fixed route around the arena to execute figure eights, a stretch of canter and small circles at trot.

Lorna rode with her eyes half shut, her body tilting to follow the carriage, listening to the pace picked out by sixteen hoofs, shadowing the routine in her mind. Nothing was forgotten.

As soon as they left the arena, Lorna jumped down and ran to the secretary's tent to await the scores. They were one point down on turn-out which had put them into fifth place but that could easily be regained. Her father had driven well, the changes of pace had felt smooth and she knew from his voice that the horses had gone steadily and not tugged for the reins.

A small crowd had gathered by the time the steward appeared with the next list. Lorna waited, holding her breath then gasped; they had lost only one more point! When the scores were tallied across the board, that put them in joint first place along with Eddie Logan's team of Cleveland Bays.

"We're equal first!" Laura called out, running across the field.

"First!" Mrs. Eden blinked and almost spilt the tea she was pouring.

"How may points in it?" Lorna's father wanted to know.

"We are both down two - Jeff

Heagney is third on four penalties and then someone I don't know at seven."

Mr. Eden clapped his hands. "Equal first! This could be our lucky day!" He picked four currant biscuits out of the tin and fed one to each of his treasures.

After lunch, Lorna and Adam exchanged their black uniforms for sturdy training shoes and well-worn jeans before helping their father re-harness the horses and climbing up behind. Their mother would watch this section of the competition from the ground. "Someone has to be around to pick up the pieces," she said.

The starter called them up to the line. The horses snorted and champed upon the loose-ring Liverpool bits. Jet pawed the ground and received a sharp reprimand.

"Three, two, one . . ." the starter counted them down.

Lorna braced her legs, gripping the iron bars that ran along the sides of the carriage and the top of the seats. She watched a drop of sweat trickle down

the side of her father's cheek and knew he was driving to win. Then, suddenly, they were away with the horses pounding down the sawdust track at a high-stepping trot.

The first hazard was easy, a gate into a lane.

"Get up!" Mr. Eden called and the lead horses spun to the left. "Steady, wait for them." The wheelers came through, bringing the carriage past the post. They were straight again.

"Away!" called her father and the

foursome sprang into canter. There were hills and banks and narrow roadways to turn along, flags to circle and sheep-pens to back into.

The water hazard was visible from a long way back, simply on account of the size of the crowd gathered around it. Lorna bit her lip, her hands tightening. If they got through this they would have a good chance of winning, but it was a difficult obstacle. She remembered how last year they had turned over in the water. Horses had a tenancy to bounce when they got into the water and then jump about and upset one another. Lorna's eyes found Cinders and she held her breath.

Mr. Eden gathered the reins and drove the horses on with his voice. They seemed to enter the water fast. A great wave of spray shot into the air around them.

"Get over! Get over!" bellowed Mr. Eden. The leaders turned sharp left and then he cried: "Come! Come!" so that they turned neatly right between two pillars in the centre of the river.

The foursome moved like a snake. The reins flicked and they were pounding away to a cheer from the crowd.

"That was fast," cried a breathless Adam. "We are in the lead so far."

Afterwards, Lorna could never be quite certain where they went wrong. Perhaps they came into the woods too fast or met the second section at too tight an angle. Perhaps it was just because Cinders thought she saw something in the bushes and shied. When it did happen it was too fast to be frightening.

One minute they were weaving between the beech trees and the next they were tumbling to the ground. Lorna's gymnastics training made her fold her legs so that she landed on her feet and immediately ran in pursuit of the carriage.

Cinders smacked her head on a low branch. She bucked and knocked into Jet who kicked out in sudden panic and hooked a leg over the traces.

Lorna ran. She caught Raven as the horses turned. Her legs took two long strides and then she vaulted onto the black gelding's back. Her knees clamped tightly beneath the collar as she leaned out to catch hold of the flying reins and pull back firmly, calling on the horses to stop.

Raven responded quickly, Eclipse soon followed suit and between them they stopped Cinders and Jet who looked about them with wide eyes.

They were trembling.

The competition was over and first place was way out of reach. The carriage was righted and wheeled slowly back to the trucks. The horses were boxed and the family made their way home.

In the horse transporter, Lorna's father was silent. Back in the yard he took Jet on one side to hose his sprained leg with cold water to reduce the swelling. Lorna fed the other horses and turned Raven and Eclipse loose. Cinders she kept aside for a while to bathe the scratches on her face and dab on antiseptic powder to help them heal.

"Will he be all right?" Lorna asked her father, pausing to stroke Jet's velvety nose.

"Just sprained himself, nothing serious," her father said and switched off the hose. "A couple of days' rest and he will be as right as rain again." He smiled gently at his daughter. "I should have thanked you earlier, Lorna. If you hadn't acted so quickly I'd have a broken leg to treat here instead of a sprain."

"Circus tricks come in handy sometimes, don't they," she teased.

Her father laughed. "I have to admit it, they do!" he chuckled. "I have to admit they do!"

Champions

Monica Stephenson dropped her satchel down to the carpet, tossed her jacket upon a waiting hook and ran upstairs, changing from her school clothes as she went. Her mind had flown ahead of her and was already bringing her bay gelding, Squib, in from the field. She had decided to take the path through the Forestry Commission land where there were lots of banks to leap. She might even find some felled timber conveniently piled at the side of the land.

"Monica!" her mother called as she picked up her riding hat from the understairs cupboard. "Come into the sitting room a minute."

Mrs. Stephenson was sitting on the settee, a letter in her lap and a cigarette between her fingers. This was unusual, since she had proudly given up smoking two years ago. Monica felt a tension rise in her throat. Her fingers curled around the polished back of her father's armchair. "What is it?" she asked.

"Daddy has to stay in Hong Kong for the summer," announced her mother. "I've decided to go out and spend some time with him, just for two months. John is happy to go to your grandparents, but of course there are no facilities for Squib there. So, I've called Aunt Hilary and she said she would be happy to take you."

The corners of Monica's mouth turned down, but she said nothing; the alternative to going to Aunt Hilary's would be to rough Squib off for the

summer and go to Hong Kong. Besides,
Aunt Hilary's was not so bad. There
would be shows to go to and good
riding around. The only real difficulty
would be her cousins ...

Three weeks later, Monica loaded
Squib along with his belongings and
her own suitcase, into her aunt's horse-
transporter. She kissed her mother
goodbye and climbed onto the transporter's passenger seat.

Once started, Aunt Hilary happily
spent the entire journey telling Monica

about her show record to date. Her special favourite this year was a strawberry roan filly foal, Coxwold First Blush, who had twenty rosettes to her credit at a mere three months old. The second foal, Elation, was not as pretty as First Blush but had more height and would be kept on for Monica's cousin, Carolyn, to ride when she was older.

Aunt Hilary generally had half-a-dozen ponies on her hands – her two brood mares with their foals at foot and a pony each for her children, Carolyn and Piers. This year, there were also two yearlings she had hung onto to break herself the following summer. Despite some misgivings about the high-handed opinions of Piers and Carolyn, Monica was soon looking forward to being at Coxwold House again and being able to learn something about the training of a youngster.

Squib was put in the schooling paddock when he first arrived to give

Aunt Hilary spent the journey talking about her show record

him a chance to get to know the other ponies without the risk of picking a fight and damaging one of Aunt Hilary's valuable beasts with a well placed nip or an iron-shod kick.

Monica stowed his tack on an empty rack in the shed and tried not to notice the rosettes that covered one wall. There were rows of simple reds, blues and yellows, double and triple coloured championships and amongst them photographs of slim-legged ponies standing perfectly beneath immaculately turned out children. Her own tack seemed chunky beside the bootlace-leather showing bridles and the flat, cut-back saddles. "That doesn't mean they can ride better than me," Monica muttered as she pushed her grooming kit under the rack.

The drawing room at Coxwold House was lined with cups and the kitchen scattered with copies of *Horse and Hound* and show catalogues. At first glance, it was an idyllic place, but Monica soon came to understand

Uncle Victor's determination not to have a single horse photograph in his study. She was glad also that she had a room of her own into which she could retreat and a door she could use to shut out Carolyn's squeaky voice extolling the virtues of draw-reins in creating the correct outline.

Generally, Monica rode out alone. The show ponies were not to jump or gallop in case they damaged their ever-so-fragile legs. Today, she flew out of the yard at a spanking trot and put

Squib into a gallop the minute his feet touched grass.

Cousin Carolyn had decided already it would be terribly funny to refer to Squib as Quid. Monica gritted her teeth and jumped her pony over the paddock fence, much to the consternation of the yearlings on the other side. On they galloped and popped out, springing high into the air and landing safely on the other side. Monica clapped Squib's neck as her temper subsided.

"Just let Carolyn try doing some real riding!" she muttered. "She'd soon understand what I meant about you being named after a firecracker if she met you out hunting, wouldn't she boy!"

Monica rode further than usual, giving the bay a long stretch across a stubble field and leaping the stacked bales. The wind caught her hair, whipped bright colour onto her cheeks and blew away the remnants of her bad temper. Squib pranced home, barely sweating and received an extra

Monica jumped her pony over the paddock fence, scattering the yearlings

scoop of maize in his feed as a treat.

Back in the kitchen Aunt Hilary, Carolyn and Piers were gathered round the table making their plans for Ainderby County Show to be held on the following day. Monica glanced at the schedule as she sipped at a mug of copper-coloured Assam tea, which was her Aunt's favourite brew.

The brood mare Spring Morning and First Blush were down for the in-hand class. Carolyn had Sapphire in the twelve-two showing and Piers his home-bred gelding Penny Black in the fourteen-two. Monica turned to look over the gymkhana games section and discovered to her dismay that the competitions were all for local Pony Club teams. "Do they accept entries on the field?" Monica asked her aunt.

"Yes, dear," she was told. "What were you thinking of? We could stay long enough for the thirteen-two jumping."

If only . . . but Monica knew her pony did not have the dexterity for show-

jumping at county level and she didn't want to spoil his courage by putting him against a course he couldn't hope to clear. "I was thinking of the showing," Monica faltered. "You haven't any entries in that class?"

Carolyn burst out laughing. "The showing classes at Ainderby are qualifiers for the National Championship, Monica!" she exclaimed. Aunt Hilary subjected her daughter to a cross look, saying: "If Monica wants to enter, then of course she can. Put

Squib in Elegance's box for the night,
Monica. You'll need to keep him clean
for the morning."

"Thank you!" Monica said bluntly
and went outside to call her pony up. "I
know you'll look smashing tomorrow,
Squib," she whispered to the bay.
"Carolyn's never seen you plaited up,
with your socks washed and your coat
gleaming. We'll wipe that smile off her
face, won't we!"

Monica spent the rest of the afternoon brushing the dust out of Squib's
coat, then soaking herself as she tipped
buckets of tepid water over his neck
and tail to shampoo them clean. While
the suds still ran off his shoulders she
fetched the hosepipe and turned the jet
on gently to wash him down and rinse
his neck thoroughly.

Squib stamped his feet, scowling at
her and he snapped to show his
annoyance. The next job was to scrape
off the excess water with the side of her
hand and throw towels over his back to
keep him warm while he dried. Using a

short-toothed comb, Monica worked her way down Squib's black mane pulling out the knots and jerking out the long hairs that would make his appearance untidy on the field.

The plaits she would leave until the morning, otherwise he would find some way of scratching them loose overnight. His tail was combed next, strand by strand. This was a time consuming job, but although she felt like skipping it, she knew it would be worth while in the end when his black tail fell from the top plait in a rippling cascade.

By the time all this was done, Squib was dry enough to groom and finally have his legs bandaged to keep them clean for the morning. In the other stables, Piers and Carolyn were hard at work on their ponies.

Monica looked over Sapphire's door to find the mare not only bandaged and rugged, but swamped by a felt hood and a long tail-guard. The only visible parts of the pony were her nose and her knees. Monica giggled.

"You've changed your mind and decided to enter the fancy dress as a clothes-horse!" she quipped. Carolyn threw a bandage at the door and sighed when it unrolled into the sawdust.

The household rose early on Saturday. For all their earlier preparations, the children set to again, brushing and polishing with soft stable-rubbers, oiling hoofs inside and out and plaiting manes which were secured with linen thread.

Once the ponies were ready, the children ran indoors to wash and change. Then, the whole assembly along with tack, brushes and wardrobe, was loaded into the transporter and they were on their way.

It did not take long for Monica to realize that she was about to make a complete and utter fool of herself. Squib's tack, for all it was clean and in good repair, was not showing standard. The leather was too thick, the saddle flaps were not cut back and she herself was the only rider without a velvet-collared black jacket.

Monica's cheeks reddened and then burned as she caught sight of Piers and Carolyn hanging over the rails and laughing. Carolyn had not won her class and had missed the qualifier but a yellow, third place rosette, was tied to Sapphire's bridle.

At the very first opportunity Monica trotted Squib out of the arena and as far from her cousins as she could.

There was another ring on the south side of the field. Monica pulled Squib to a halt as she watched six workmanlike ponies show off their paces. "What class is this?" she asked a woman standing by the rails. "The Working Hunter Pony," Monica was told. The woman patted Squib's neck and gave Monica a smile. "If you hurry you will still have time to enter him in the under fourteen-hands class," she said.

The competiton ran in two sections – first, a jumping course over medium-sized rustic fences and then a flatwork session to show the ponies' paces and obedience. The ponies had more substance than those in the showing ring. Two were being ridden with martingales and amongst their riders there was a selection of black, blue and tweed jackets. Monica felt her nerves recede and she sat deeper and more confidently in the saddle.

Squib was the last pony to jump. Monica rode into the arena and pushed him into a canter just as the loud-speaker announced Piers had won second place in his class. The fences came quickly. Monica jumped them at a hand gallop, directing Squib to the centre of each, confident of his ability.

Ten ponies went clear and filed into the ring for the second section. Monica scrutinized the performances of the riders before her and opted for a simple show; cantering on each lead, a burst of gallop, then coming quickly back to hand and performing six steps back-reining.

Squib set off at a sprightly pace. He took the gallop eagerly, but came back well. Monica bit her lip, concentrating hard as she dropped her weight into the saddle to ask for a square halt. She then teased the reins, touching lightly with both heels to keep Squib's quarters straight as he paced backwards.

The judge asked the class to lead round the ring at a walk and looked over her notes, conferring with the steward. Out of the corner of her eye, Monica saw Aunt Hilary, Piers and Carolyn at the rails and her stomach gave a nervous twist. The judge moved her hand. Monica glanced round to see who had won and realized she was being waved in. The judge patted Squib's neck and handed Monica a red rosette.

"You realize of course that you have qualified for the National Championship, don't you!" Aunt Hilary pointed out, as she congratulated her niece.

"I have?" exclaimed Monica. She laughed and flung her arms round Squib's neck. "I'm sure Sapphire and Penny Black will win a different qualifier," she said.

Beating Carolyn and Piers no longer mattered to her so much. That single red rosette meant so much more – it meant that, even without the daintyness of a show pony or the bouncing stride of a showjumper, Squib had the makings of a real champion!

The Search

"So you mean to say that none of the horses at Johanna's are any good for dressage?" exploded Anka Gronbach, sounding as though she could hardly believe her ears. Her friend, Heidi, nodded. She was sitting cross-legged on the linen chest, her long fingers wrapped around a mug of steaming coffee and generally feeling very cold after the walk to Anka's home.

"Not even Dagaz?" asked Anka.

"He's much too bossy," Heidi told

her. "In the arena, he would hurry everything and kick up a fuss when I asked for a movement he didn't like doing. He's good with you because like you he enjoys jumping. He likes the thrill of speed and dressage would bore him."

"He does have a point!" joked Anka. "I know we have to do flatwork, but I wouldn't bother if it didn't improve Asta's jumping."

Heidi reached for a cinnamon and honey biscuit. Her eyes rested on the trail of photographs across the bedroom wall showing Anka and her black mare, Asta, clearing a wall, then parallel bars and finally stretching over a water jump.

"It's true," she admitted. "Dressage is hardly something to do for excitement but it does have a special kind of satisfaction. It's wonderful when the horse suddenly understands the movement you have been asking for and the test flows smoothly. It's like finding the perfect dancing partner."

"*You cannot speak with the horse, but for sure, harmony between the rider and the horse can be very deep,*" said Anka, quoting Reiner Klimke, world dressage champion and Heidi's absolute hero. "You must have told me that a hundred times. It does happen in other sports you know. Asta and I have a special relationship and that's why she puts in so much effort if I mess up on the approach when we jump."

Heidi forced herself to smile, though her heart was sinking. Anka could rely on her horse, because jumping was straightforward.

The dressage arena had no prompts. The horse relied upon its rider to tell it what was required. It had to be a special horse, one that was obedient to command, but full of pride and panache. Inwardly, Heidi sighed. If Anka could not understand, how could she hope to explain to her father the sort of horse she must have.

He would have preferred her to take up jumping, like her friend. He understood jumping. In competitions, it would have been easy for him to understand why she won. The proof would be there in front of him – a clear round in the fastest time.

Instead, she had to try explaining that the dressage test had fifteen movements and each was marked for accuracy and flow, while all the time he made jokes about her top hat falling onto her nose.

There were three trots to be performed faultlessly. Working trot, in which she entered the arena, the far-reaching extended stride and the collected trot with its short, bouncing movements in which she had to execute a perfect circle.

Her father thought dressage belonged in the circus ring. Sometimes she thought he would take her *there* to find a horse. It was three months now since Heidi's first horse had been sold. Since then, the arguments had grown sharper. Last night her father had said it was costing him more in petrol to look for the horse than it would be to buy it.

Heidi's hand closed, snapping the biscuit and showering her jeans in crumbs. They had better find one tomorrow, she told Anka. If not, she felt sure her father would refuse to look any more.

The following day dawned fine with a clear blue sky. Heidi turned her face to the sun as she carried warm crispy buns back from the bakery for breakfast. The air was balmy and crocuses pushed purple and gold heads up beneath the apple trees. The sense of spring gave her new hope.

The journey up the autobahn was long and tedious in the stuffy atmosphere of the car. Heidi followed the route on a map and when the car turned onto a country road she sat forward, looking out for the high roof of the indoor school and the rows of loose-boxes.

Herr Schulmann was waiting for them and came to meet their car. He was a tall, smartly dressed man with a thin moustache that ran along his upper lip like a pencil line. "So, this is the young lady who wants to be a dressage champion," he said after they had all made their introductions. "Let us see what we can find for you."

He clapped his hands and a young woman in dark jodhpurs and a blue sweatshirt appeared from the tack room. "We will run Madrigal, Suzette, Adler and Runnwar loose for Fraulein Bergen to see their paces," ordered Herr Schulmann. He turned to Heidi and her parents, beckoning with his hand: "This way!"

The indoor school had seating along two sides and mirrors hanging at the corners and the centre lines for the riders to check their positions and that they were riding straight and able to prevent the horse from wavering.

The first horse, Madrigal, trotted across the sawdust. Her neck arched beneath a row of tiny braided plaits. Her tail had been pulled to lift cleanly from her quarters like a shimmering banner. Each of her legs had been wrapped in white bandages from fetlock to knee to show off her stride more vividly.

The groom flicked a long schooling whip and Madrigal struck into an easy canter. "Beautiful mare," Herr Schulmann said to Heidi's father. "Twelve years old. She has won many classes already. A true lady's mount."

Heidi sat on the edge of her seat. The mare moved well. She had a kind expression. She was proven in competitions. But something made her hold back. She was still not sure.

Of the other three horses, only one caught her attention. He was a tall, black gelding with a bold expression and proud manner. He had the presence to command attention in the arena, but he bucked persistently and there was a lot of white in his eye. Heidi was not sure she would be able to manage him.

It did not take long in the saddle to

have her answer. The black horse nipped the groom when she helped Heidi into the saddle. He poked his head forward to steal the bit and swished his tail in resistance when she tried to collect his paces. It would never work. He was fighting her all the time.

Madrigal was like an angel to ride after the gelding. She flexed her head readily to the curb rein. Her transitions were smooth up to trot and into a rocking horse canter. Heidi brought her right heel back as they came across the centre and felt the mare's back swing underneath her as she changed the lead of her canter. At a touch of rein or heel the mare stopped, started, walked backwards and turned on her haunches.

When Heidi walked back to the bench her father was smiling, certain their quest was at an end. Heidi shook her head.

"She doesn't suit you?" Herr Schulmann blinked, having felt sure the mare was sold.

"Looked great to me – you won't find a better horse than that," Heidi's father said, nodding at her meaningfully.

Heidi bit her lip. He was warning her that it was Madrigal or none other, not unless she went off and found the horse herself. There was nothing wrong with the mare. She was well schooled, but ... something was missing! Heidi could not explain it, even to herself, but her instincts told her riding like clock work was not what Reiner Klimke had meant by '*harmony*'.

Heidi walked into the yard ahead of them. Disappointment ached in her chest. Now, she felt they would never find a horse. She took a breath and sniffed back the tears welling in her eyes. She was about to turn to Herr Schulmann to thank him for his time, when her eye caught that of a bay mare in one of the loose-boxes and her heart stood still.

"Could I look at that bay?" she asked, her voice quavering.

"Osterei? Of course," said Herr Schulmann, "I did not think of her. She has not had the training of the others. She is just a riding horse, but if you would like to try her, of course you may."

The mare was bright bay with black dappling across her shoulders and hindlegs. Her ears were a trifle long, her cheekbones broad. Her eyes were kind and dark and her legs firm with strong, low joints.

Heidi's legs began to shake as she

watched the bridle and saddle go on. Common sense told her she was being reckless. If the mare was going to be any good at dressage Herr Schulmann would have seen the potential long ago.

Back in the school, Heidi took up the rein and touched the mare's sides. She moved off into a long striding walk. Her ears flicked forward and back, inquisitively. At a touch she was in canter, her head up, pulling a little, very eager. She was not highly schooled but she could become so. Something seemed to click into place in Heidi's heart as she brought the mare back to walk and she understood for the first time the *harmony* she was reaching for. Then, she looked to her father and nodded. They both knew that the search was over.